KU-265-672

This Little Tiger book belongs to:

_____

_____

_____

A Very Merry Christmas

Maudie Powell-Tuck ★ Gill Guile

LiTTLE TiGER

LONDON

It was Christmas Eve at Bramble Cottage
and everything looked perfect.
Baubles twinkled on the tree,
holly hung from the mantelpiece
and a fire crackled merrily.

But something was missing.
  "It just doesn't feel like Christmas,"
sighed Mr Mouse.

"I know what we need,"
said Mrs Mouse.
"A Christmas party!"

So they pulled on their boots and
scurried off to invite their friends.

There was just time to bake
some biscuits before they heard
a KNOCK! KNOCK! KNOCK!
at the door.

"Merry Christmas!" cried Fox.
"Look what I've made. You can't
have Christmas without
a dinosaur cake!"

"What a good idea!" said
Mrs Mouse.

"Dinosaur cake at Christmas?"
squeaked Mr Mouse. "Are you sure?"

Just then, there was
a RAT-A-TAT-TAT!

"We've brought our piano," said
Mr Beaver. "Christmas just isn't
the same without beaver carols!"

"Get ready, everyone," added Mrs Rabbit.
"Here come the kids!"

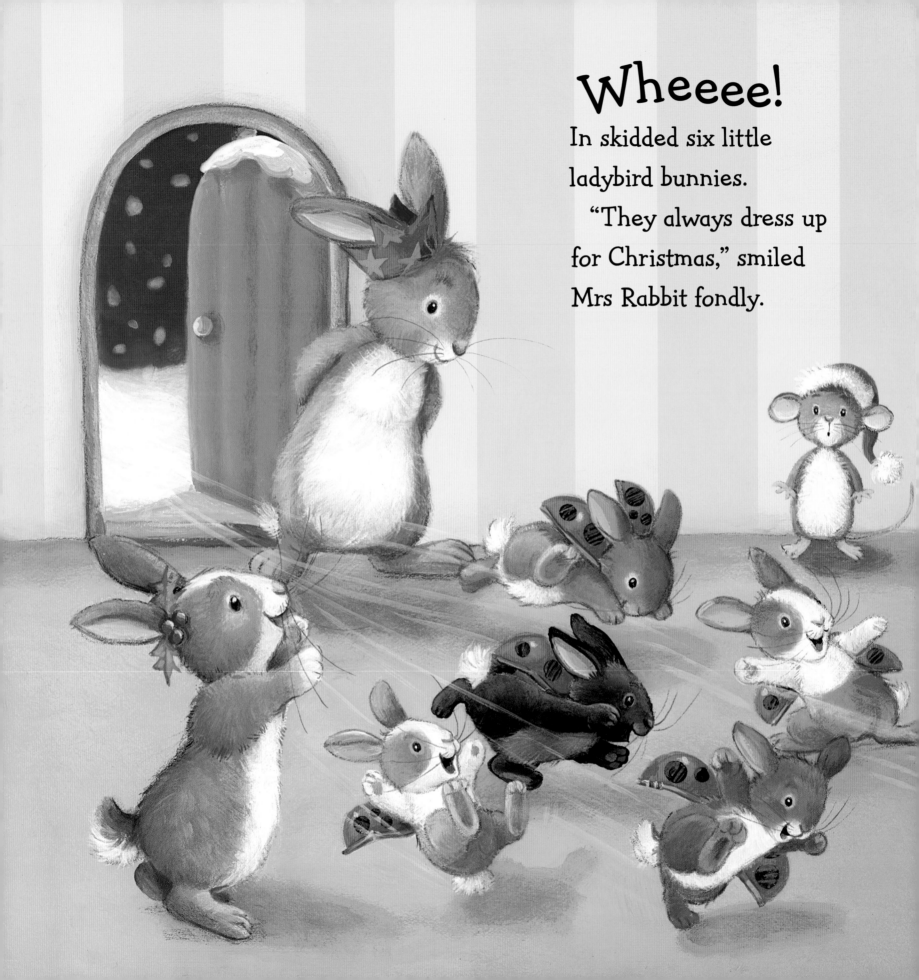

Wheeee!

In skidded six little ladybird bunnies. "They always dress up for Christmas," smiled Mrs Rabbit fondly.

Then Mrs Beaver struck up a tune.
"Deck the dams with mud a-plenty,
Fa la la la la, la la la la!"
"Goodness!" squeaked Mr Mouse.
"Are ladybirds and mud Christmassy?"

DING DONG! went
the doorbell.

"I hope I'm not too late," said Bear. "I couldn't find a big enough cactus. It's not Christmas without a cactus."

"Hooray!" everyone cheered.

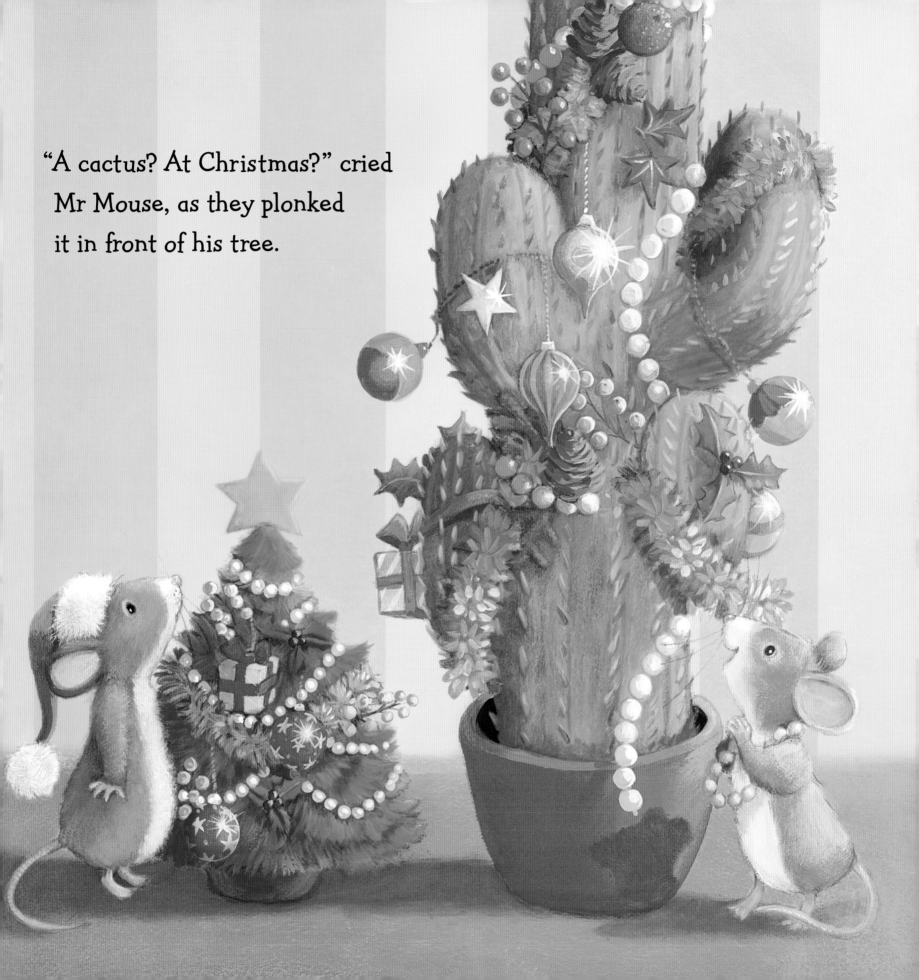

"A cactus? At Christmas?" cried
Mr Mouse, as they plonked
it in front of his tree.

"Enough!"

wailed Mr Mouse. "Cactuses, dinosaurs and ladybirds just AREN'T right! This isn't like Christmas at all!"

"But darling," said Mrs Mouse,
"everyone is having such
a great time."

Mr Mouse looked around.
Bear was dancing with
the ladybird bunnies . . .

Fox had joined in with
the beaver carols . . .

and Mr Rabbit had already eaten far too much dinosaur cake.

Mr Mouse began to smile.
It was a little bit silly.
It was a little bit odd.
But without a doubt, it was . . .

. . . the most wonderful Christmas ever!

For Mutti Bear x ~ M P T

For my wonderful husband and best friend, Andy x ~ G G

LITTLE TIGER PRESS LTD,
an imprint of the Little Tiger Group
1 Coda Studios, 189 Munster Road, London SW6 6AW
Imported into the EEA by Penguin Random House Ireland,
Morrison Chambers, 32 Nassau Street, Dublin D02 YH68
www.littletiger.co.uk

First published in Great Britain 2014
This edition published 2020
Text by Maudie Powell-Tuck
Text copyright © Little Tiger Press Ltd 2014
Illustrations copyright © Gill Guile 2014

Gill Guile has asserted her right to be
identified as the illustrator of this work under
the Copyright, Designs and Patents Act, 1988
A CIP catalogue record for this book is
available from the British Library

All rights reserved · ISBN 978-1-78881-888-9
Printed in China · LTP/1400/4682/0422

3 4 5 6 7 8 9 10